May all your
dreams come true!
☺ Tara Anne Carposano Malia

The Special Princess

outskirtspress
DENVER, COLORADO

Dedicated to my Mother and Father, Nicholas and Stephanie Campasano...
You have always been my sunshine and the wind beneath my wings. A wise
man once said, "Parents' love is whole no matter how many times divided."
(Robert Brault) Who I am today is because you love each of us so wholly and
unconditionally. You never stop giving of yourselves, even now that we are all
grown up. I hope you know I love you with all that I am.

Outskirts Press, Inc.
http://www.outskirtspress.com

PAPERBACK ISBN: 978-1-4327-3831-0
HARDBACK ISBN: 978-1-4327-7627-5

Outskirts Press and the "OP" logo are trademarks belonging to Outskirts Press, Inc.

PRINTED IN THE UNITED STATES OF AMERICA

Holmdel usually stays pretty quiet and calm...until the day BLACKY arrived! Hi! I'm Tara, and I live with my family in a town called Holmdel. There are friendly neighbors in Holmdel, and they smile a lot when people pass. Everyone takes care of one another. The kids play together at the swim club during the summer time, and we're in all the same classes at school. Too bad Blacky tried to ruin everything!

Blacky was a terrible, mean witch! She wore a long, black cape and her hat pointed like a needle in a haystack! Blacky loved to scare people by flying around on her broomstick. She spoiled the nice, blue sky by blackening it with the smoke trailing behind her as she flew. Blacky even resembled a broomstick because her hair exploded messily from her head and her body could be used as a toothpick! Blacky's menacing face and BIG, hairy wart on the very tip of her nose even scared the bats and birds as she soared through the air. Her crooked and broken-toothed frown frightened the people of Holmdel so much that everyone stayed at home, safely tucked in their homes. Kids stopped having birthday parties and even the police force seemed afraid. Blacky had to be stopped! But, how?

Blacky rode around town on her broom for hours. Anyone who ran the risk of going out immediately ran back to their homes at the sight of Blacky! Even people driving in cars had to hide in garages whenever Blacky flew high in the sky. Blacky was so mean she decided to eternally keep the town captive. If anyone dared to venture out when she was around, Blacky cast a spell on them: "Bibbity, bobbity, boo, I will cast a spell on you...frogs and toads and lizard lips, here's my potion, take a sip. Dare to try? Dare to come out? I'll make you cry, I'll make you pout! So stay inside! I make the rules! If you do not listen you are a fool!" Then, Blacky's cackle and babble could be heard across town, hurting the townspeople's ears. The people of Holmdel did not know what to do.

One day, I had enough of running away in my own town, so I decided to find my friends to play. I figured, maybe if I ignored Blacky, she would scram! So, off I went...then she spotted me and started to speak, "Hello, Tara. How nice of you to come out and play. I was beginning to get lonely. No one except you has left her house for days...I just don't know why..."

"Blacky, no one comes out because you bully them! Leave me alone! Let me go play with my friends! You don't scare me!" I yelled back at her, even though she did scare me, really!

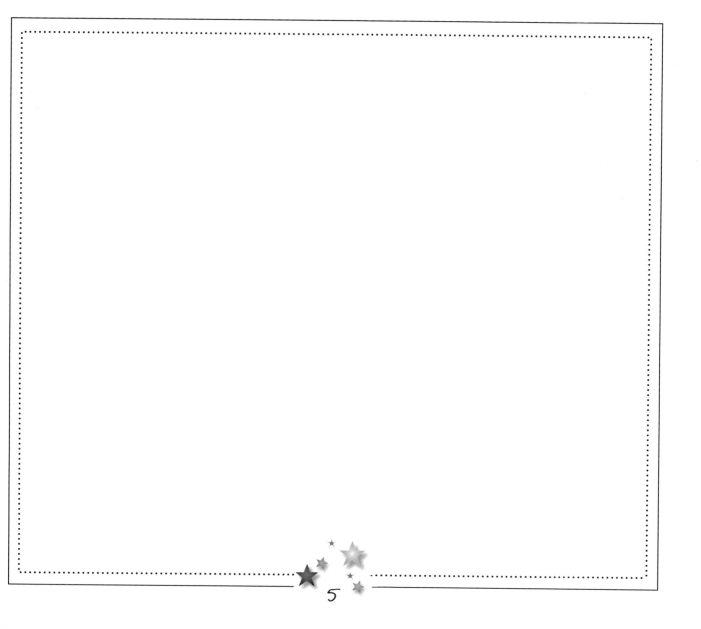

Well, now Blacky boiled with anger. No one ever stood up to her before! Blacky's surprise made her powerless, and she didn't know what to do! All of a sudden, her ugly face scrunched up and her black, crooked teeth poked from her mouth in a humongous frown. Before she disappeared, she made a nose dive on her broomstick, heading right toward me! I started running, because I didn't want to be Blacky's dinner in the bat cave, but I stopped when I heard a loud shriek. When I turned around to find the noise, I realized that Blacky screamed and disappeared into thin air! Wow! I made her vanish! I figured out her secret! ...Blacky could be stopped for good...with a little help! When I told my siblings I almost got captured, my sister, Nicole, told me Blacky was causing more commotion in town, and no one would even go to the food store! My brother, Vinny, said that he couldn't race cars with his friends either. We decided that we had to stop this witch! The three of us had to come up with a plan. We ventured outside and decided to find our friends for some help. If Blacky did see us, at least we'd be together this time! Vinny, Nicole, and I made it safely to town, but now we had to find our friends without getting spotted. Being outside was risky, but we had to do it! We walked carefully, hiding behind trees and parked cars.

We were almost at our destination when Blacky spotted us! We started to run, but Blacky was still mad at me from before, so she swooped down at lightening speed and caught us all. Blacky carried us away on her broom and took us to her secret cave. Luckily, Blacky fell asleep before she locked the doors, so we snuck out before she woke up. Boy! That was a close call!

Once we finally made it home, Vinny, Nicole, and I talked and talked and finally figured a way to stop Blacky. We created a foolproof plan, but we needed more help... we'd need the whole town to work together.

Since Blacky tangled her broomstick in all the telephone wires, we couldn't even tell people our idea by calling on the phone. What would we do now? Lickety split! Vinny found another way to communicate with everyone. He'd send a note to all the neighbors, describing our plan. His trusty remote control car would deliver the scheme from house to house, until each person heard the news:

NOTE: PROJECT TOP SECRET — HELP GET RID OF BLACKY! EVERYONE MEET OUTSIDE AT 5:00 PM TOMORROW NIGHT. DO NOT BE LATE! WE HAVE TO DO THIS TOGETHER, OR IT WILL NOT WORK! ONCE YOU'RE OUTSIDE, CLOSE YOUR EYES AND HOLD HANDS. THEN SAY TOGETHER, "GO AWAY, BLACKY! WE'RE NOT AFRAID." SAY THOSE WORDS OVER AND OVER AGAIN UNTIL BLACKY DISAPPEARS. THIS WILL WORK, BECAUSE BLACKY'S SPELLS DISAPPEAR WHEN PEOPLE STAND UP TO HER. WE HAVE TO SHOUT LOUDLY SO SHE FLIES AWAY IN SURPRISE!

Okay...here it goes! The car traveled from house to house until the entire neighborhood knew the plan. Soon, the news spread across town and all we had to do was wait for tomorrow...

Tomorrow arrived...I stepped outside first, at exactly 5:00 PM. Blacky saw me and immediately chanted a spell. Before she could finish, the townspeople came from their houses and shouted, "Go away, Blacky! We're not afraid! Go away, Blacky! We're not afraid! Go away, Blacky..." Blacky's surprise made her shriek in horror. The people of Holmdel spoke louder and louder, until no one could even hear Blacky's screams. She shriveled up and disappeared into thin air, leaving only a trail of black smoke behind. We won! Blacky left for good, and Holmdel could only celebrate...or so we thought.

Everything in Holmdel seemed back to normal. Kids celebrated birthdays, children played outside and grown-ups went back to work. Finally, my birthday came, and I decided to have a great, big party! Now that Blacky didn't bother us anymore, nothing could stop the party. I just couldn't wait to be ten years old!

I awoke the day of my birthday and had a funny feeling in my stomach. Something weird was going to happen, but what could it be?

The day dragged with nothing unusual happening at school, not even any birthday cupcakes. Humpfh! When I came home, my mom told me we would be going to my favorite restaurant for dinner before my party. My excitement made me happier, but my nervousness only grew. Before I could figure out why I was so giddy, we arrived at the restaurant. To my surprise, the whole restaurant came alive with pink ribbons and streamers. Music blared all around and all my friends jumped out and yelled, "SURPRISE!" What a great birthday! This was the best birthday EVER! And I thought everyone at school forgot! Not a chance!

The next day being a little boring after such a great birthday, my brother and sister decided to come with me to seek an adventure in the woods. We wanted to find a secret place for a new clubhouse. We walked and walked for almost one whole hour. We were so tired we decided to rest on a bunch of old tree stumps. The stumps looked kind of strange, but they were perfect chairs so we could rest our tired feet. Each stump sat so neatly that the three formed a perfect triangle. The triangle reminded me of Blacky's horrible hat, but I quickly thought about happier things and forgot her with a shudder. "Hey!" I shouted. These stumps could be a perfect place for our secret meetings! Just when we all agreed that the stumps would be the official place for our clubhouse, the forest shook violently. The stumps quickly sunk into the ground, even before we could stand. The ground swallowed us up when all of a sudden, we noticed a magical crystal cave, leading to the most beautiful house we had ever seen. We couldn't believe our eyes! The whole house was built with real jewels and diamonds that sparkled just like a ring! Everywhere we looked, the pearls and diamonds blinded us and shone in our eyes...

My brother, Vinny, said not to go any further, but we just had to see what was inside...We held hands and knocked on the door. No one answered, but the door swung open all by itself...creepy...but I went in first, anyway.

As soon as I walked into the house, everything sparkled more brightly than ever, like magic! Once we were inside, we felt unusually comfortable, like we were supposed to find this magical palace. As we stepped into the living room, we found a beautiful mantle made of swirled marble. Each room cascaded into more and more spaces, like a labyrinth, and the house went on and on and on… each compartment making us more curious than the last. The gigantic size of the house made it possible to have elevators and escalators, which wrapped in shapes like candy canes at the North Pole. The banisters sparkled so brightly that I could even see my reflection in the millions of jewels! We explored the fourth floor of the house and found yet another stairway, a special, spiral staircase that lead up into the clouds, wrapped in ribbon all the way to the sky! At the top of the stairs sat a glass door, probably leading to another secret chamber.

We climbed the stairs, and to our surprise, a magical robot named Rosie greeted us and welcomed us to her home. Rosie was as lovely as her house, because she wore a crown that glimmered like the wand of a princess and her cheeks were smiling and pink. Rosie had been living in this secret palace for one hundred years without any visitors. We were her first guests, and she happily let us use her palace for our secret clubhouse. We asked Rosie all kinds of questions…"How did she get here? Where was she from? Who built her house?" Rosie's friendly smile turned to a smirk. She wouldn't answer any of our curiosities. She only told us this, "The house is magical. You cannot tell a single soul about it or about how you found it." We promised Rosie we wouldn't tell. Rosie also showed us an old, crinkled, yellow note pinned to the wall of the house. It read:

CAUTION! IF ANY GEM IS REMOVED FROM THIS HOUSE,
IT WILL LOSE ITS MAGIC AND DISAPPEAR, FOREVER!
BE WARNED!

Vinny, Nicole, and I carefully maneuvered throughout the house, not touching any of the shining jewels. We promised Rosie we'd keep a special watch over her palace, and we'd protect her from any intruders. We had to go home for dinner, but we told Rosie we'd return tomorrow. She reminded us not to tell anyone our new secret, and to make sure no one followed us to our new hideout when we returned.

We finally arrived at home, just in time for mom calling us to dinner. Our excitement took away our appetites, so after supper, we tried to rest, but we couldn't wait for after school tomorrow when we'd see Rosie again. Mom asked us all kinds of questions, but we were sworn to secrecy...

The next day arrived and school crawled on and on. We impatiently awaited the time we could visit our new clubhouse. After what felt like an eternity, school ended, we arrived home, and changed into play clothes. Mom just smiled and told us to be home for dinner. We agreed, and raced to our stumps in the woods. We sat upon them, and sure enough, the ground shook and we found ourselves back at the magical cave leading to the jeweled house.

As soon as we headed towards the palace, we realized we had been followed. We tried to hide, but it was too late. A woman appeared behind us, saw the magical palace, and immediately ran towards the jewels. "Stop," we screamed! "You can't take any jewels from this house, or it will lose its magic and disappear!"

The woman looked up, and cackled a question, "What are your names?" For some reason, she looked oddly familiar, but we couldn't decide why. She told us to call her "Mrs. Smart" because she knew EVERYTHING! We didn't want her to follow us inside, but we had a feeling she already knew what the inside held, too. We had to figure out a way to lose Mrs. Smart, but how?

Mrs. Smart didn't say too much, but she smiled a crooked smile that chilled our bones. We couldn't decide what she wanted or why we recognized her, so we ran inside to ask Rosie for help. Rosie didn't want Mrs. Smart to know about her palace, so she grew more and more nervous, remembering all that we told her before about Blacky coming to Holmdel. Rosie told us to be especially careful of Mrs. Smart, because Mrs. Smart sounded even smarter than we thought! Actually, Rosie thought Mrs. Smart might be Blacky in disguise...

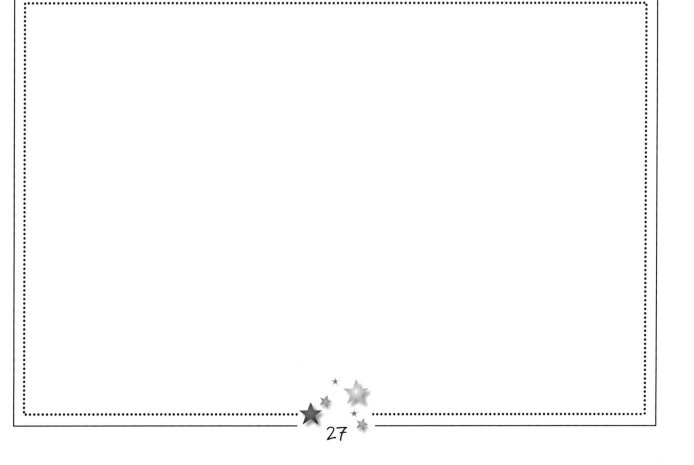

That's why Mrs. Smart's smile seemed crooked! Blacky revisited us undercover! Oh, no! Not again! We told Rosie we would not return until we discovered a plan to get rid of Blacky for good. We didn't want the house to disappear and we didn't want Rosie to get hurt.

After dinner that night, strange things began happening in Holmdel. The wind felt as brisk as December's breath, even though it was only October. The chill in the air bit as sharply as an arctic wind. Instead of pretty red leaves appearing on the trees, they turned immediately from green to black, and the moon stayed full for two whole weeks. Blacky didn't appear again as Mrs. Smart, but everyone knew she was near. We felt her presence in the air.

One day, darkness descended immediately after sunrise. Even the sun grew tired of pushing the gloomy clouds away! All of the schools in Holmdel dismissed the students early because the parents of the town believed Blacky would appear on this dreary day. Sure enough, they were right. At 6:00 PM, a huge, puffy swirl of black smoke appeared in the already gray sky. Blacky was back, and she was as mean as ever! Although we feared Blacky, we knew if we didn't overcome her evil, Rosie and our new palace would be destroyed forever. So, my brother, sister, and I invited Blacky into the forest by sneaking away from our home and luring her into the woods after us.

Blacky believed she had all the power, so she accepted our challenge. Little did she know that she would be the one to be ZAPPED! Of course, Mom wouldn't hear of letting us play outside, so we knew if she learned what we were up to, we'd be in BIG trouble. We were determined to win anyway, and have the town of Holmdel restored to safety, once and for all.

Mean people stink, so Vinny, Nicole and I thought we'd teach Blacky how to be good. That way, Blacky could be nice to herself and even make friends! We thought that maybe if Blacky felt the love and the magic of our special palace, she could be transformed from a spiteful bully into a special princess. We just had to believe our plan would work. We needed the sparkle of our clubhouse and the faith in our hearts to change Blacky, the mean witch, forever.

As we approached our stumps, we felt Blacky's breath lingering closely behind us; she grew more and more impatient. Blacky didn't know our destination, so she started cackling under her breath. She seemed to become more and more awful as we walked more deeply into the dark, evening forest. We were soooo scared, but we had to stand up to her! We were almost there...she had to keep following us...for just a few more steps...finally, we reached the stumps.

Blacky now seemed amused at our adventure because she recognized the stumps as the way to the jeweled palace. She thought we would turn over the palace to her! Boy, was she in for a surprise! Our plan was risky, but it had to work...

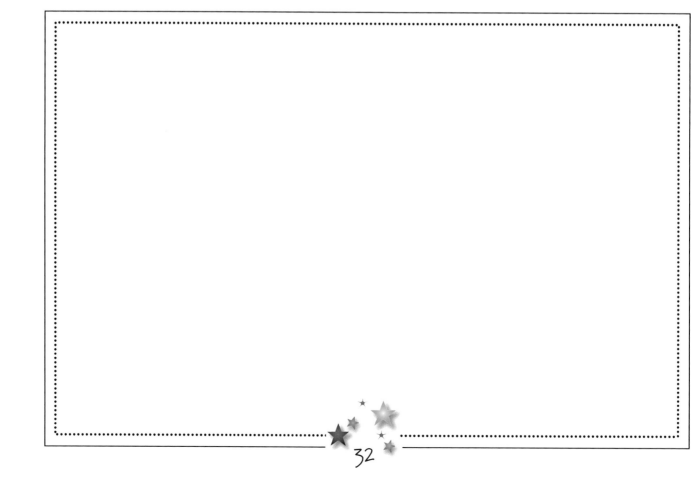

As soon as we grew closer to the house, Blacky squirmed. She grew uncomfortable and appeared to be weakening. We invited Blacky inside the cave entrance; then, entered the house. She must have known that we had a plan, because she tried to use her evil powers to carry the house into the sky. Once we all gathered together in the living room with Rosie, the house started to rumble and shake. It rose from the ground and Blacky's cackling spells grew louder and louder as the house flew higher and higher into the sky! Then, something wonderful happened. Vinny, Nicole, Rosie and I took each other's hands. We closed our eyes and imagined good thoughts. We told each other how much we were loved. We remembered the power of our magical house and started smiling. The house spun and rose faster and faster, until a bright flash in the sky forced us to open our eyes.

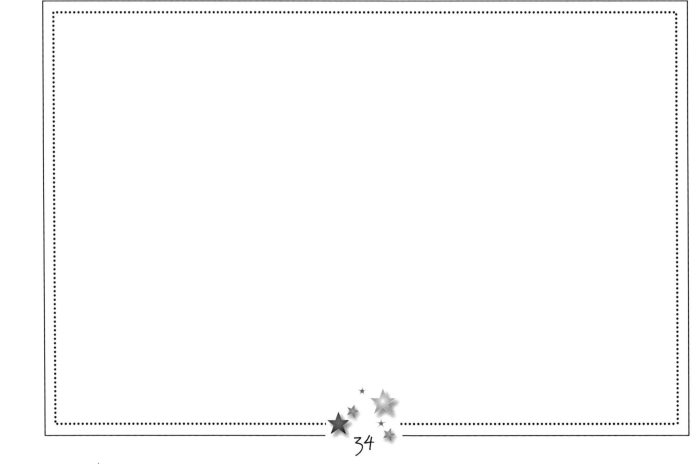

The magical house and our belief in its powers turned all of Blacky's evil and ugliness into beauty and wonder! We couldn't believe our eyes! Blacky was now dressed in a pink frilly dress with puffy sleeves. She wore lots of lace and sparkles that glittered every time she moved. She wore a splendid crown of gold and held an enchanted wand that poured lingering streams of pink and gold wherever she waved it in the air! Most importantly, she smiled a beautifully genuine smile! Blacky was now the prettiest good witch we had ever seen! She glimmered more brightly than our palace when she smiled and promised to watch over the people of Holmdel, forever.

The black leaves and smoke-filled sky magically transformed back to the lovely, auburn colors of autumn. The birds sang songs, trees and flowers bloomed unseasonably, and our troubles were swept away with Blacky's enchantment. Even Mom excused us from being grounded since our plan to bring Blacky into the woods worked! We still visit Rosie today, and no one else has ever tried to find her magical palace. Even Blacky, now called the Special Princess, promised to keep Rosie's secret, forever.

CPSIA information can be obtained
at www.ICGtesting.com
Printed in the USA
LVIW020742030812

292799LV00002B